To Lowell, Lee and Chelsea

I Love My New Toy!

Mo Willems

WALKER BOOKS
AND SUBSIDIARIES
LONDON · BOSTON · SYDNEY · AUCKLAND

An **Elephant & Piggie** Book

Hi, Piggie!
What are you
doing?

6

I love
throwing toys.

Zip!

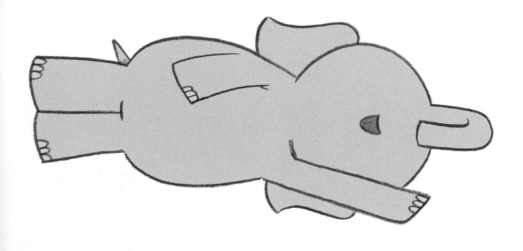

Turn

Here it comes!

ZOOM!

BRE

21

You broke my toy.

24

29

No!
My new toy
is broken!

36

AAAAA!

AAAAA!

Cool!

You have a
break-and-snap
toy.

SNAP!

Enjoy!

BREAK!

SNAP!

BREAK!

SNAP!

I want to play with you.

Friends are more fun than toys.

THIS **Elephant & Piggie** BOOK
BELONGS TO:

_____

_____

_____